God Loves Me More Than That

Dandi Daley Mackall
illustrated by David Hohn

WaterBrook
PRESS

God Loves Me More Than That
Published by WaterBrook Press
12265 Oracle Boulevard, Suite 200
Colorado Springs, Colorado 80921
A division of Random House Inc.

Scripture quotations are taken from the Holy Bible, New International Version®. NIV®.
Copyright © 1973, 1978, 1984 by International Bible Society. Used by permission of Zondervan
Publishing House. All rights reserved.

ISBN 978-1-4000-7316-0

Text copyright © 2008 by Dandi Daley Mackall

Illustrations copyright © 2008 by David Todd Hohn

Published in the United States by WaterBrook Multnomah, an imprint of The Doubleday Publishing
Group, a division of Random House Inc., New York.

WATERBROOK and its deer colophon are registered trademarks of Random House Inc.

Library of Congress Cataloging-in-Publication Data
Mackall, Dandi Daley.
    God loves me more than that / Dandi Daley Mackall ; [illustrations by David Hohn]. — 1st ed.
        p. cm. — (Dandilion Rhymes)
    At head of title: Dandilion Rhymes Series
    Summary: Simple, rhyming text explores the extent of God's love, which is more than the bumbles
in a bumblebee and softer than a kitten's sneeze.
    ISBN 978-1-4000-7316-0
    [1. Stories in rhyme. 2. God—Love—Fiction.] I. Hohn, David, 1974– ill. II. Title.
    PZ8.3.M179God 2008
    [E]—dc22
                                        2007050514

Printed in the United States of America
2008—First Edition

10 9 8 7 6 5 4 3 2 1

And I pray that you, being rooted and
established in love, may have power,
together with all the saints, to grasp
how wide and long and high and
deep is the love of Christ, and to
know this love that surpasses
knowledge—that you may be filled to
the measure of all the fullness of God.

—Ephesians 3:17–19

How much love does God have for me?

More than the letters between *A* and *Z*.

More than the bumbles in a bumble bee.

God loves me more than that!

Tell me, please, is the Lord's
love high?

Higher than the moon
in a starless sky!

Higher than a space shuttle flying by.

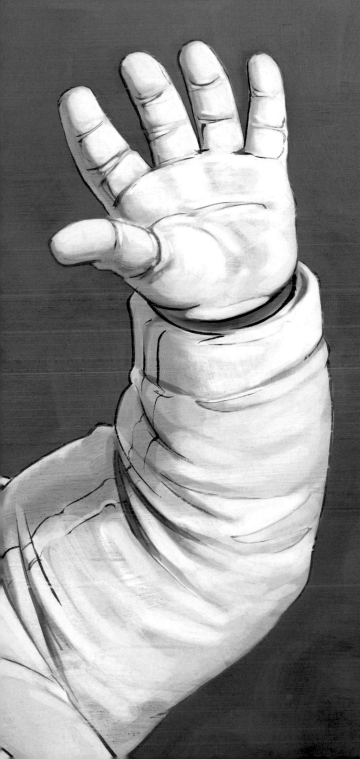

God loves me higher
than that!

Just how deep is God's love for me?

Deeper than a treasure chest beneath the sea.

Deeper than a wishing well could ever be.

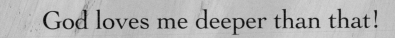

God loves me deeper than that!

Tell me, please, is the Lord's love wide?

Wider than a semitruck
from side to side.

Wider than the prairies where the cowboys ride.

God loves me wider than that!

Just how much does
the Lord's love weigh?

More than elephants munching hay.

More than hippos on a rainy day.

God loves me bigger than that!

Tell me, please, is the Lord's love loud?

Louder than the cheering of a football crowd.

Louder than a thunder-rumbling,
storm-charged cloud.

God loves me louder than that!

Is God's love soft? Won't you tell me, please?

Softer than the sigh of a summer breeze.

Much, much softer than
a kitten's sneeze.

God loves me softer than that!

Lord, it's great to be loved by you.

Hope you know that
I love you too.

Nice to know that my whole life through,

God loves me more than that!